Poetry
In
Motion

By

Jane Rowe

Jane Rowe

Jane Rowe

Jane Rowe

DEDICATION

TO MARTIN C. HODGSON, WHO HAS TIRELESSLY HELPED BY
USING HIS EXTRAORDINARY TALENT TO CAPTURE BEAUTIFUL
PHOTOGRAPHS

Jane Rowe

CONTENTS

Jane Rowe

ACKNOWLEDGEMENTS

To all my friends who attend my poetry night, Vanessa, Lizzy, Amanda and Ann for the use of her Pub, the Cock Tavern in Downham Market

Introduction

Poetry in motion, is a modern, fresh, young, look at poetry, in an easy to read format. Ms Rowe wrote, "The enemy within," at the tender, age of fourteen, when her battle with mental health started. Her life long suffering of insomnia, led to her writing poems as a means of expression.

For many years, Jane lived on benefits, ill both physically and mentally, her mother dead, what family, left, turning away. In and out of hospital, every thing climaxed, after her marriage broke down, post natal depression, setting in, Lucy her young daughter living with Jane's ex husband.

Against the odds, Jane Rowe's, health complaints, all became controllable, finally, in her forties, a complete person. When walking back from late night swimming, one hot summer, this author thought of the story format for her first novel, "The Desolation of Silence!" The idea snowballed, encouraged, by her partner, Martin Hodgson, it became a published E book.

Since then Jane has written a sequel to her first book, which will be a trilogy, an alien story, "Luna," a contemporary take on extraterrestrials psyche, a children's book, with her daughter, Lucy Rowe, who got the writing bug, after being in the local paper, with her mother. Her book is called, "The Flying Cat!" All of her torment, became something meaningful, what had been a curse for years, inspired and drove Jane.

The plight of the young mentally ill, she saw in hospital, made Jane, vow, to some how give back, at some point, to help, young girls, who might fall ill, to see you can progress, come off benefits, look attractive, even on medication, become empowered. Yes Jane has mental illness, but yes, she is an inspiring figure, as is her partner, Martin, who did all the camera work in this anthology

Jane Rowe

Jane Rowe

The Enemy Within

Heart beating,
Disturbed, mad,
Battling, battling
The eternal fight
To make wrong right
The grim reaper rises from his grave,
My soul he doest want to save
Am I a lunatic?
Pain, pain, locked
In my rushing, rushing mind
This is the ride, vibe
I run, run, run
From the reaper
Is this me?
Or insanity?
Not right in the head
Told I am better off dead
His bony fingers on my neck
I trip, he is gaining, gaining
Unstable, unbalanced
But I race ahead, free
He smiles, at me with a ghastly grin,
Stating, "I will return and I will win, because I am the
enemy within!"

(written age 14)

Jane Rowe

Photographs

I try to remember
The hot burning
The sad, sick yearning
But only can recall
A shadowed history
A untrue photographic memory
Of you
My first love, last love
Forever love!

Jane Rowe

Nirvana

My bruised and scared body trembles so much
Wanting, not wanting
So afraid

Of damaging what is concealed inside
Of burning and turning
Going out of my mind

Yet it is worth the risk, as I stand on the precipice
The drop is sheer
In your arms I feel no fear

I see a glimpse of heaven
On the other side
As I walk, you catch me, I am so blind

Yet I can see
So slow
We have far to go

Take me to nirvana
Be gentle, so gentle
Yet, be firm, be harder and harder and harder
I purr
I am not the blonde gentleman prefer!

Jane Rowe

Father

I longed for you to see
The suffrage in my soul
Yet bitter sweet tears I cried
When we achieved that goal
You wandered in the reccesses
How I wanted to never leave you
Never leave you
But in the end I had to grieve for you
The tear and the bond of blood
We shared, as I wallowed in despair
Knowing you always cared
Close, yet apart,
Father, you are always in
My heart

Hawaiian Girl

I used to think I was an Hawaiian Girl
Wearing a hula skirt, like a Polynesian
Eyes closed, lost in daydreams
I felt the warm breeze, like a caress
Even on a cold day
Motionless, I travelled away
Feeling the vibe
So happy to be alive
With my long dark hair
Making garlands of flowers
Alone in the garden for hours
Listening to shells
Enjoying the simple idea
Of being, being in an imagery tribe
So proud, vibrant, exited to be alive
Blossoms in my hair, so happy
To live in my inner Hawaii

Jane Rowe

Inside your mind

Past and present collide
I think I can see inside your mind

I feel, I feel I have met you before
Who would have thought
I would walk through your door

Desire, compassion my life passes before me
Is it déjà vu?
Am I old, young do I love you?

Emotions cascade
Is it hate or love
I cannot decide

Oblivion

I want to think of nothing
Be nothing

Floating, floating, with the ebb and flow
Swirling, just becoming a mist
To be invisible, to not exist

Elusive, out of reach

Bound by chains
My wish for oblivion is all that remains

Jane Rowe

Meat

You gather near
Of you I have no fear

Diseased and rotting
My flesh putrid
Yet you love the taste

So sick, so fresh decomposing alive
Yet my suffering, decay makes you survive

Miserable in my final moments
Which is prolonged and prolonged
So bad, so good, never know right from wrong

Wrong, right, you eat and eat and eat
Until in suffering I am gone
Then to fresh meat you move on

Jane Rowe

Like a butterfly

Beautiful,
So exquisite
You're a butterfly
How I would like
To be you, so happy
Carefree,
Joie de vivre
Yet so soon to die
You live for the moment,
That moment, that
Never stops,
Starts or finishes
But just enjoys
And enjoys and enjoys
Hedonistic bliss
So sweet, like nectar
The distilled essence
Of a first kiss
How do I get to this?
 Tears of blood I cry
With wings of battered
Dreams I fly
Will I ever get there?
Will I get there?
Do really care?

Winter

So frozen
The season, afraid of the cold
Like death; time suspended
Suffocating, growing old
The frigid, unwelcoming, aloof, storm
So icy, chilling. Glassy
Enchased, ice, deceased,
Rigor mortis set in, you will never be warm
 Ice turned into threads
A frozen waterfall
Pure transparent
The peace of the dead

Jane Rowe

Pieces of me

I scream inwardly
I doubt, I shout, silently
Wish I could learn quick
Then I would not get sick
Things I have seen, unseen
Wish I could live, like
The American dream
I try and try, to patch
The jigsaw together
To make the happy ever
After forever
My heart breaks with out a
Sound
 I think there are pieces
Of me all over the ground

Look behind the Smile

We look but do not see
Because we live in a visual society
If people glanced under the skin
Discovered the masked spirit within
Like hundreds of glistening beams
We are all not as happy as it seems
Brain washed from the beginning
Commercials, flashing, saying, talking
No questions asked just accepting
What we are told to be
Does a happy meal really make us happy?
Does it really matter if you are not a size zero?
Just be your hero
All different and diverse
This trend for same, same, same
We must reverse
Turn off the T.V and close your eyes for a while
Maybe then you'll sense your inner smile

The System

The system, the system that contains,
Contains the pressure, pressure,
Cooks us alive,
Making us fight each other, to survive
Forced to work on a assembly line
Making us pretend
When we are sick, to be fine
Take our kids away
Paying the price
Of a down trodden life
Have your own flesh and blood
Twist the knife
This is the voice of grit, pain, dirt
Suffering
Fearing, fearing
Having no home
Not money, for even a phone
The system, that turns us against,
The us, in us,
United we stand, divided we fall,
To rebel, is like banging your head,
Against a brick wall!

Blood

Blood is thicker
Than water
But you turn away
From me and my daughter
This is my body
This is my blood
Holly sacrilege
Walk to church
We would love to see your new house
For Lucy to meet your spouses
Where has the bond of blood gone?
Surely I have not killed anyone!
I am not perfect
I admit
He who throws the first stone
Don't be such a hypocrite
Turn, turn from blood
Praying to a god above
In my book brother and sister
Should stick together,
Not have a miss understood, feud forever
Forgive thy enemies
As they forgive you
Lets make peace
I love you still
A life lived in fear
Is a life half lived
Blood, my blood, your blood, my
Blood, is inside you
Oh brother be true
How ever hard you try
How ever much about your forgotten family you lie,
Tears of blood I cry, Lets all try together
Love, forever
Blood, my blood
Is your blood

Race

Race crime on the increase
Why can't we just make peace?
One race,
The human race
I had a dream
I have a dream
The pen mightier than the sword
Youngsters of all colors winning awards
Lets come together
Together
Peace, love, forever

The rush

The rush
The burn
Rushing, shadows
Flittering, racing
Pacing, faster
Faster,
I want it to stop
I want it to never end
I want to be my own best friend
So hard to love myself
When I despises my lying eyes
Until, I almost
Hurt, hurting, destroying
My sickness
Yet is it?
I am different
Just different
Not a danger
To any stranger
How do I know
The secrets, everyone holds inside?
Diverse, complicated, polluting their own minds

Jane Rowe

Outside Inside

People come and people go,
They only come to see the show
After the curtain falls,
They never answer my calls
Never going to get away from it all
The ghosts of my past
Are here to last
Why is live like a game of hide and seek?
Why is my future oh so bleak?
They always tell me your ok,
But in the night
They go away,
Shadows slipping, slipping by,
Only me alone to cry,
Outside, inside the
Dark thoughts stay,
How ever close you think you are
Your always miles away,
People judge a book
By its cover,
The real person they never try to discover,
Outside inside, the dark,
Thoughts stay,
However close you think you are your always miles
away

Jane Rowe

Suicide

Fatal, extreme,
Always hope, threw out,
Pale, pallid, rumination,
Under, under water,
Sickening fast,
You want to die,
This attempt will not be
Your last,
We are all human, mortal,
Passing, temporal, transient,
Transitory,
Yet I lived to
Tell my story,
Never knew the heart ache,
I brought to Mum and Dad,
Conversations rushing, that I wish we'd had,
Remember what ever,
Catastrophe, collapse,
Rise above, rise threw the fog,
The weight, that drags,
Always believe in your self,
Dust to dawn,
Ignore the storm,
Do not try to die!
That is what I cry!

Jane Rowe

Love

What is this word
That I cannot say?
Is it what I see in
Men's eyes everyday?
No that is lust
With as much value of dust

(Written age 16)

Schizophrenia

Schizophrenic girl,
Told your out of your mind,
Your not,
Your one of a kind!
I know your forgotten, schizophrenic girl,
Institutionalized too young,
Before your life, had just began.
Just because your hearing voices,
Doesn't mean in life you have no choices.

The boundaries, between fact and fiction blurred,
Doesn't mean things can't improve,
I know you can be what you want to be!
I know you can be what you want to be!
I know you can be what you want to be!
Don't be frightened;
Learn, push, keep fit!
Your not just a social misfit!

Jane Rowe

Mother

Affectionate
Caring
Your heart taught me about sharing.

When I was sick
You changed the sheets
Unbreakable, soft hearted
Emotion still raw
Turbulence inside
I hope you never saw

I miss you more than words can say
Wish you had never
Gone away.
But dear mother
I cannot deny
The knock out punch
When you stopped breathing
I never stopped grieving.

Glad you did not live
To see your family at war
Those words that hurt
Treating me like dirt.

I feel you watching from afar
In the twilight
From an enchanted star
Your words of forgiveness
Echoing inside
Making me hold onto the remnants
Of my tattered mind

I wish, I wish that you were still alive
Never knew anyone so kind
Because I will never find another
I will always be at one with my goddess mother.

Jane Rowe

Jane Rowe

The writing on the walls

Do you believe,
Believe in love that never leaves,
You touched what was untouchable
Known you for years,
Who would have known
Your would calm my fears
Saw the method
In my madness
Saw the pain, the hidden sadness
Intrigued by the writing on the walls
You answered my frightened calls
The lies they said, you know were untrue
Always knowing I love you.

Matrix

Life's bloom is death
Push myself through the pleasure and pain
Again and again
Am I insane?
Is it in my brain?
I struggle, push, I struggle
Will it all be too much?
Will I cry?
Will I die?
Fate tosses and turns me in her wheel
What cards will she deal?
Good or bad?
Sane or mad?
I think my head will break like an egg
Will I go under?
Survival, survival of the fittest
Is that magic?
Questions, questions, questions?
I do not have the answer
I don't care
I should really have married a millionaire!

Jane Rowe

Locked

The pain is deep
I do it in my sleep
You try my locked door
The less I want it
Makes you want it more
I would like to run
I like to hide
The door is locked
But I'm locked inside

Voices

I hear you.
I hear you
No one else can
Stop telling me what to do
Like a brain storm
You keep me warm
Like a fire
I perspire
Voices unspoken
Unsaid
Are hurtful
These voices in my head
You whisper like a lover
Like a friend
Telling me it's the end

Jane Rowe

Déjà vu

Oh daughter
You say you want to die
My soul is wailing
Oh why, oh why?
Am I a bad mother?
Spinning,
Spinning back in time
Remembering how my mum suffered when I had a bad time
Déjà vu
Am I her, it's not you
Treading in her steps
Where angels fear to go
Please, please
Remember I love you always
The burning, yearning, brand
You hold my heart in the palms of you hands

Jane Rowe

Padded cell

Muffled, pushed around
Never stood on solid ground
Overdoses, common place
Life in disgrace
Blood on my hands
Life swirling like the sand of the promised land
Mirage ahead
Scream and scream
Yet not a sound heard
Crying and crying
If this is living
What is dying?

Jane Rowe

Misfit

Blond, brunette
Drinking to forget
The knife, the life
Scratch, scrape
Hiding rape
I suck, suck so deep
Half awake, half asleep
Cannot stop this artificial mess
Wish I could change my psyche like a dress
Slip out of this worn out gown
Take away my frown
Flicking, flicking, flick
Vomit, taste, smell the sick
I am blond, am I?
Eyes, red, incased
Black tears I cry In peace I rest
Go away, I tell that darkness
In which my soul is processed.

Mind Out

Bitter sweet memories
Tears
Leaves falling
Death and survival start of
Winter calling
Frost bite
I cry into the night

Jane Rowe

Autumn

You come to me with
Your sweet, cool caress
Turning, turning
With your frosty hand
You undress
But this is temporary
Transit, radiant
Colors dying
Caught in
The eternal circle
That does not stop
Just rolled around
And around
Bittersweet
Grieving death, reborn

24/7

I went without sleep
 For 24 hours
I went to the gym
For my showers
Every pore, every thought of you
I hardly eat
But somehow did not lose weight
Tears behind the veil
Masking emotions
Can never fail
Spin, spin in circles dance and sing
Just wanted to go back to when
Your life began
Turn off the heating at winter time
Do not commit a crime
When the sun goes down
And cannot be seen,
It is still warm
Hidden, obscene
Of doubt
I shout
The fairy tale clock twisted
Around myself, becomes invisible
Crawl, crawl over broken glass
Cut, hurt
True inside
Just anxiety, pride
The roulette wheel spins
When your numbers up you really know
Could be you
Who knows what happens tomorrow

Marilyn

Jane Rowe

We never met
And never will
Because you swallowed
That fatal pill
Covering up what
Was mentally ill
Blond, platinum, girlie, strawberries and cream
You spun, weaved dreams
 Upon the silver screen
Taking the damage
Desolation, pushing away tears, frustration
In my teen age years
Looking at your
Cheese cake pictures
I feel your fears
Satin, silk
Your pale epidermis
Tasting of milk
I wanted to be you, to be you
Tangled, broken
The bond unspoken
dumb blond, Dumb brunette
Clever, stupid, cleverly stupid
Many memories you wished to forget
Dying alone
Never having a proper home
Loved, lost, turbulence, your soul burned,

For that maternal bond you yearned
So sorry, so sad
Happy days you rarely had
Complex, you bleached your hair
Didn't wear any under wear
 Longing, long for someone
To teach you
A daddy that would be true
Like a spider caught in its
Own web
The nirvana you created left you
So cold, so dead

Jane Rowe

I love you

I watch your dark head
As you sleep
You are Keanu Reeves
I am Brittany Spears
Have we really been together
All these years?
Feels like yesterday
Is today
With old eyes
That feel brand new
I say those three words
I love you

Jane Rowe

Jane Rowe

In My bed

With pink lips
And gentle whisper
Pure, new, crisp
I feel your newness
Cotton sheets
Brand new
I will always be true

Jane Rowe

Daisy

You came to me one day
In the garden you would
At first stay

Your big slanted eyes
Looking so surprised
We found fun together
The bond, unexpectedly clever
So fluffy, pure
Feline
Kitty cat
Your little paws led you
To my house
Daisy you rewarded me
With a mouse
Those who owned
You did not see
What I did
Playing like two kids
Having our
Girlie sleep over's
My cat best friend
You were once left in the frost alone
Do not worry
You will always have a wonderful home!

Jane Rowe

New Year

Exercise
Keep fit!
Buy all the gear
Push, join the gym
Jump, jump, swim
Don't eat carbs
The battle of the bulge
Try and win
But don't worry if it gets too hard
Don't fear
There is always next year!

Jane Rowe

Birthday

Coming into existence
Anxiety of birth
A happier, fresh start
Reborn every year
Celebrate, celebrate
Send out your cards don't be late
Wrap up the gifts
Tie up the ribbon
Have a surprise, open your eyes
Its your birthday today

The Lucy Poems

Introduction

This is a set of poems, by Jane Rowe, inspired by her daughter, Lucy, who Jane's has a close bond with.

Suffering from post natal depression, Ms Rowe had a period, when she did not see her daughter, in that time, becoming engrossed in her writing again, after year of not being creative. As much as this period, was dark, the light came in Jane's world, by the exploration, of the written word.

Lucy is also, an Amazon published author, of a children's e book, "The Flying Cat!" With her mother, which they both loved producing. Lucy has started another book, which she would like to be a paper back, but she has fallen off the wagon of writing for the time being, just enjoying the simple pleasures of being a child, her mother not taking away her child's, innocence, allowing her breathing space, to grow emotionally.

The poems are simple, the most thought provoking, is, " Your Eyes as Blue as the sky's." Not long after Jane started to see her daughter again, after a few months apart, Ms Rowe, noticed a new sadness in daughters eyes. The title came to Jane as little Lucy, absorbed in her mothers nail varnish, said, "They are as blue as the sky's!" That night Jane Rowe, came up with the concept, of the poem.

Jane hopes you enjoy, these poems and the pictures of Lucy which go along with the text. Lucy stated she wanted her pictures in the book, liking the idea.

Poem for Lucy

I would like to watch you laugh and play
I would like to be with you every day
To wash your skin
And put your sleepy
Body to bed
To feel you nestle
With your drowsy head
With your long dark hair
And your full pink lips
I love you from
The top of your head
To your toe tips

My Little Girl

My little girl,
So grown up, poise beyond your years
On the cusp of innocence, never feel my fears

My little girl
Hope you met your prince charming one day
That for you he never goes away

Build your castles made of sweet talk
Do not let them fade
I do love you, don't let them tell you I am bad,
I am just sad, maybe a little mad!

Pregnancy

Inside me you flutter
Like a butterfly
So happy you make me
Want to cry
The flower of my womb
I am the sun, you
Are my innocent bloom
Every breathe, I take
You take with me
Happiness grows, every day
From my thoughts you are never far away
Together we are one
Yet separate
I look forward to your birthday

Jane Rowe

Reborn in you

When you were born
I was reborn too
Through your eyes
I saw the world
Look brand new
Innocent delight
You saw in everything
Happiness you could
Only bring
People would turn
And look and stare
At you so happy
Without a care
How ever near or
Far
Fate will never
Tear us apart

Jane Rowe

Jane Rowe

Your Eyes As Blue As The Sky

I see the suffering within your eyes,
So new, so mature
As blue as the skies

Complicated, diverse,
Convex, no voice, no say,
When you were born only seems like yesterday.

Unanswered questions, unanswered questions,
You see what is unspoken, what is beneath,
I weep at your tiny feet

Your orbs, azure, cobalt,
In them I dive so deep,
Inarticulate sounds,
I shed the tears you weep

Just to feel, to feel, the beatitude,
Deep, deep inside
Your eyes, my eyes, so blue, so blue, as the skies

Jane Rowe

FIN

Jane Rowe

Notes

Notes

Jane Rowe

Notes